# MY BEST FRIEND'S
# BANGLES

THUSHANTHI
PONWEERA

ILLUSTRATED BY
MAITHILI JOSHI

SIMON & SCHUSTER BOOKS FOR YOUNG READERS
NEW YORK   LONDON   TORONTO   SYDNEY   NEW DELHI

My shadow stretches ahead of me as I cycle to school.
Soon one shadow becomes two.

It's my best friend, Divya!

Divya and I are alike
in so many ways.
We both love to play
dress-up,

we both love to eat
pittu (with sugar!),

My amma

and we both miss our ammas.

Divya's amma

Both our mothers live far away, in a country so hot, it's a desert.
They work for families who pay our mothers to cook, clean, and babysit.

We receive the money they
earn once a month . . .

. . . although we only see them once a year.

It's hard not having
Amma home all the time.

But I have Divya
and she has me.

The morning sun warms us as we cycle downhill. We stop to wave at the village aunties, whose chatter fills the air, when . . .

CLiNK! CLiNK!

"Whoa! Where did you get those from?"
Divya's eyes glow. "They're rainbow bangles from Amma."
"She sent them by mail?" I ask.

"No, she brought them herself!
She came back yesterday!"

"Oh."

I'm still smiling on the outside, but
my heart falls with a thump,
my throat forms a painful lump,
and my eyes begin to sting like they do
when I peel onions to help Appa cook.

Why is Divya's amma back and not mine?

At school, the bangles are all I hear and see. Their rainbow colors remind me of Amma.

CLINK! CLINK!

The deep-red powder she smeared in the parting of her hair.

CLINK! CLINK!

The shiny orange saree she wears in the picture I keep under my pillow.

CLINK! CLINK!

The fragrant yellow dhal she cooked every day because it was my favorite.

CLINK! CLINK!

The old green suitcase she packed to the brim when she had to go.

CLINK! CLINK!

It's hard to be happy about the bangles when they make me feel this way.

Divya doesn't notice.

During recess, I get as far away from the bangles as possible. Even if it means not sharing my food with Divya like we always do.

Maybe she will come looking for me.

She doesn't.

All because of those bangles.
Those too-bright, too-loud,
too-everything bangles.

Finally, Divya notices me.
"Don't you want to try them on, Selvi?" she asks.

CLINK!
CLINK!

"No, thank you."
"Why not?" Divya replies.

These rainbow bangles are
starting to make me see red.

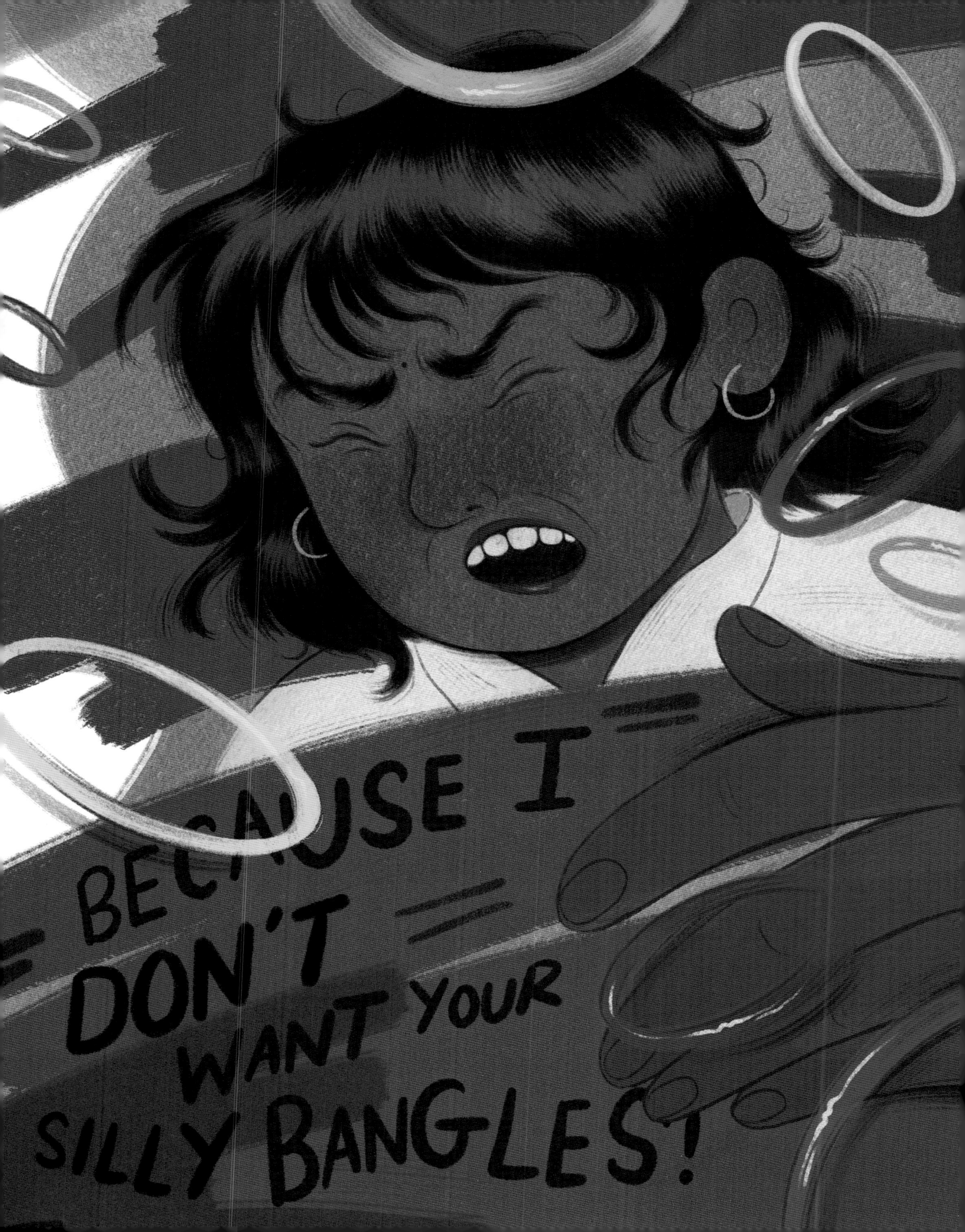
BECAUSE I DON'T WANT YOUR SILLY BANGLES!

"Look what you've done, Selvi!"
Divya shouts, chasing after the bangles.

The red inside me fades
and my cheeks warm up with shame.

The days that follow are extra long. Extra lonely.

Will Divya ever want to be best friends with me again?

I need to apologize.

I'm almost at her house when I hear loud
peals of laughter coming from inside.
It must be Divya and her amma.

Maybe they're playing dress-up
or eating pittu with sugar.
She doesn't need *me*.

A soft drizzle slows my ride back home.
Not even my shadow keeps me company.

Suddenly . . .

It's Divya!

"Selvi, wait! I want to talk to you."

As Divya gets closer, the lump in
my throat gets bigger and bigger.

"I'm sorry for throwing your bangles, Divya," I say.
"I just wish my amma came back too."

Divya doesn't reply. Instead, she reaches into her pocket.

"I'm sorry too," says Divya.
"Now we'll each have our own rainbow for gloomy days."

Her voice is only a little louder than a whisper.
I know what that voice means.
"Is your amma going back?"
Divya nods.

Then, just as the sun bursts through the clouds, Divya smiles. "But *your* amma will be back soon. You'll share her presents with me, won't you?" she asks.

"Of course I will," I say. "Because we're . . ."
"Best friends," we say together.

Our favorite song blares out of a passing tuk-tuk.
We get on our bikes, singing loudly.

The bangles are nice, but my real rainbow . . .

. . . is Divya.

# AUTHOR'S NOTE

Sri Lanka is famous the world over for its Ceylon tea. During the nineteenth and twentieth centuries, the British, who were the colonial rulers of Sri Lanka at the time, brought down laborers from South India to work on the tea plantations here. Referred to as Estate/Malaiyaha Tamils, these laborers endure harsh living conditions to this day. Tea pluckers, who are usually female, are paid less than ten US dollars a day. Their houses, often just a single room, are provided by the estate owners and are called "line houses" because they are set in a row and share a single roof. The workers can never own them, only live in them and pass them down to the next generation, making it hard to leave the system.

Selvi and Divya are fictional characters, but their story could very well be a real one. Due to the inability to make ends meet, tea pluckers like their moms leave their families behind to be domestic workers in other countries. Although this allows them to provide for their families financially, the void left in the lives of these young children growing up without their mothers is immense. As I write this note, Sri Lanka is going through its worst economic crisis, compelling even more mothers (and fathers) to leave the island and find employment overseas.

As a mother, it pains me to witness a society that compels a child to be separated from their parents. This story was written in hopes that the future will see these children empowered, given the freedom to explore life beyond the one they were born into, and able to break the cycle of poverty.

To learn more about and help children like Selvi and Divya and the
marginalized communities they live in, please visit the following websites:

MJFFoundation.org
TeaLeafTrust.com

To all the mothers who miss their children, and to all the children who miss their mothers.
And to Dhevan and Rahya, my eternal rainbows.
—T. P.

To my lovely grandmothers, Malini and Veena. Though we never met, you are missed.
—M. J.

SIMON & SCHUSTER BOOKS FOR YOUNG READERS • An imprint of Simon & Schuster Children's Publishing Division • 1230 Avenue of the Americas, New York, New York 10020 • Text © 2024 by Thushanthi Ponweera • Illustration © 2024 by Maithili Joshi • Book design by Chloë Foglia © 2024 by Simon & Schuster, LLC • All rights reserved, including the right of reproduction in whole or in part in any form. • SIMON & SCHUSTER BOOKS FOR YOUNG READERS and related marks are trademarks of Simon & Schuster, LLC. • Simon & Schuster: Celebrating 100 Years of Publishing in 2024 • For information about special discounts for bulk purchases, please contact Simon & Schuster Special Sales at 1-866-506-1949 or business@simonandschuster.com. • The Simon & Schuster Speakers Bureau can bring authors to your live event. For more information or to book an event, contact the Simon & Schuster Speakers Bureau at 1-866-248-3049 or visit our website at www.simonspeakers.com. • The text for this book was set in Garamond. • The illustrations for this book were rendered digitally. • Manufactured in China • 0224 SCP
First Edition
10 9 8 7 6 5 4 3 2 1
Library of Congress Cataloging-in-Publication Data
Names: Ponweera, Thushanthi, author. | Joshi, Maithili, illustrator.
Title: My best friend's bangles / Thushanthi Ponweera ; illustrated by Maithili Joshi.
Description: First edition. | New York : Simon & Schuster Books for Young Readers, [2024] | Audience: Ages 4–8 | Audience: Grades K–1 | Summary: Two friends experience jealousy for the first time when one of them is gifted a set of bangles from her mother.
Identifiers: LCCN 2022053295 (print) | LCCN 2022053296 (ebook) | ISBN 9781665921718 (hardcover) | ISBN 9781665921725 (ebook)
Subjects: CYAC: Best friends—Fiction. | Friendship—Fiction. | Working mothers—Fiction. | Emotions—Fiction. | Sri Lanka—Fiction. | LCGFT: Picture books.
Classification: LCC PZ7.1.P6433 Rai 2024 (print) | LCC PZ7.1.P6433 (ebook) | DDC [E]—dc23
LC record available at https://lccn.loc.gov/2022053295
LC ebook record available at https://lccn.loc.gov/2022053296